P9-CPZ-314

This book belongs to:

_____

_____

_____

First published by Walker Books Ltd.,
87 Vauxhall Walk, London SE11 5HJ

Copyright © 2002 by Lucy Cousins
Lucy Cousins font copyright © 2002 by Lucy Cousins

Based on the audiovisual series *Maisy*, a King Rollo Films production for
Universal Pictures International Visual Programming. Original script by Andrew Brenner.
Illustrated in the style of Lucy Cousins by King Rollo Films Ltd.

Maisy™. Maisy is a registered trademark of Walker Books Ltd., London.

All rights reserved. No part of this book may be reproduced, transmitted,
or stored in an information retrieval system in any form or by any means,
graphic, electronic, or mechanical, including photocopying, taping, and
recording, without prior written permission from the publisher.

First U.S. edition 2002

The Library of Congress has cataloged the hardcover edition as follows:

Cousins, Lucy.
Maisy cleans up / Lucy Cousins. —1st U.S. ed.
p.   cm.
Summary: Maisy the mouse and her friend Charley clean her
house together and then treat themselves to cupcakes.
ISBN 978-0-7636-1711-0 (hardcover)
[1. Cleanliness—Fiction. 2. Mice—Fiction. 3. Friendship—Fiction.] I. Title.
PZ7.C83175 Mad 2002
[E]—dc21   2001035479

ISBN 978-0-7636-1712-7 (paperback)

11 12 13 14 SWT 20 19 18 17

Printed in Dongguan, Guangdong, China

This book was typeset in Lucy Cousins.
The illustrations were done in gouache.

Candlewick Press
99 Dover Street
Somerville, Massachusetts 02144

visit us at www.candlewick.com

Maisy Cleans Up

Lucy Cousins

CANDLEWICK PRESS

Maisy is cleaning her house today.

Ding-dong!

Someone is at the door. Who could it be?

It's Charley!

He's come for a visit.

He can help
Maisy clean!

Charley smells something delicious in the kitchen. He's hungry.

Oh, look — cupcakes!

But the floor
is still wet.
Charley has to wait
until it's dry.

While he's waiting, Charley puts the toys away.

Maisy vacuums
the living room.

Then Charley washes
the windows from
the inside . . .

and Maisy washes
them from the
outside.

That looks better!

At last the kitchen floor is dry.

Now Maisy and Charley can have some cupcakes.

Hooray!

Good job, Maisy.
Good job, Charley.
Treats! Yum, yum!